BLUFFALO

Wins His Great Race!

Babette Douglas

Illustrated by
Barry Rockwell

Kiss a me™ ♥
Productions

Kiss A Me™ Productions, Inc. produces toys and booklets for children with an emphasis on love
and learning. For more information on how to purchase a Kiss A Me collectible and plush toy
or to receive information on additional Kiss A Me products, write or call:

Kiss a me™ Productions

Kiss A Me Productions, Inc.
90 Garfield Ave.
Sayville, NY 11782
888 - KISSAME
888-547-7263

About the Kiss A Me Teacher Creature Series:
This delightfully illustrated series of inspirational books by
Babette Douglas has won praise from parents and educators alike.
Through her wonderful "teacher creatures" she imparts profound lessons of tolerance
and responsible living with heartwarming insights and a humorous touch.

BLUFFALO Wins His Great Race

Written by Babette Douglas
Illustrated by Barry Rockwell

ISBN 1-89034-377-7
Printed in China

www.kissame.com

To *Theresa M. Santmann,*
Who "buffaloed" me into writing this story

The new buffalo baby
Struggled to rise,
To lift himself up
To his biggest size.

His mother stood proudly
And nuzzled his neck.
"You'll be the pride of the herd,
One they won't forget.

"For now you must rest
And be nourished each day
And practice to lead them
During skirmish and play."

To the leader she led him,
To show him with pride.
"Here's the son you've awaited
Who'll run at your side."

The great buffalo stood silent
And studied with ease
This tiny new buffalo
Trying to please.

He thought he was standing
As straight as a tree.
He instead stood shaking
And knocking at knee.

" 'Twas only hours ago
I newly arrived,
But already I know
I can run at your side.

"I'm straight and I'm strong,
And I'm ready to go.
I know you are old,
So I'll start out real slow."

The great buffalo was startled,
Shock showed on his face.
"I'll run this young upstart
All over the place."

They started out running,
The old and the new,
Each rushing to show
What each one could do.

The ground shook below,
From the giant beast's speed.
He covered the ground
With miles he wouldn't need.

And the buffalo baby?
He ran an odd race!
He struggled and puffed
To keep up the pace.

The great giant turned
And ran all the way back.
The baby never noticed.
He thought his win was a fact.

Back at the finish,
Again side by side,
Something was amiss!
Something no one could hide.

Instead of both facing
The end of the run,
The baby was still facing
As the race had begun!

The herd that was watching
Laughed out with glee.
"That babe's look of victory
Is funny to see."

The baby stood gleaming
With pride on his face.
He announced to those gathered,
"I've won my first race!"

His mother with wisdom
Stayed silent and still.
His father said laughing,
"You have or you will?

"But the heart of a winner
Is brave and is true,
And these are the gifts
That I see, son, in you."

The herd stamped all together
To show they agreed,
Then circled their youngest
Who someday would lead.

And the medal they gave him?
Not for winning the race,
But for the *effort* he gave
To running in place!

Now...

Even snails can win a race,
No matter what your view.
Much depends on effort given
That tests the winner in you.

THE END

Babette Douglas, a talented poet and artist, has written over 30 children's books in which diverse creatures live together in harmony, friendship and respect. She brings to her delightful stories the insights and caring accumulated in a lifetime of varied experiences.

"I believe strongly in the healing power of love," she says. "I want to empower children to see with their hearts and to love all the creatures of the earth, including themselves." The unique stories told by her "teacher creatures" enable children to learn to recognize their own gifts and to value tolerance, compassion, optimism and perseverance.

Ms. Douglas, who was born and educated in New York City, has lived in Sayville, New York for over forty years.

Additional Kiss A Me™ teacher-creature stories:

**Character toys are available for each book.
For additional information on books, toys,
and other products visit us at:**

www.kissame.com